ABC
PASSOVER
HUNT

B is for Blessings: Jacob, Boyd, Sloan and Jane - T.B.

For my wonderful family with love - H.P.

Text copyright © 2016 by Tilda Balsley
Illustrations © 2016 Lerner Publishing Group, Inc.

KAR-BEN PUBLISHING
A division of Lerner Publishing Group, Inc.
241 First Avenue North
Minneapolis, MN 55401 USA
1-800-4-KARBEN

For reading levels and more information, look up this title at www.lernerbooks.com.

Library of Congress Cataloging-in-Publication Data

The Cataloging-in-Publication Data for *ABC Passover Hunt* is on file at the Library of Congress.
ISBN 978–1–4677–7843–5 (lib. bdg.)
ISBN 978–1–4677–7848–0 (pbk.)
ISBN 978–1–4677–9612–5 (EB pdf)

Manufactured in the United States of America
1 – CG – 12/31/15

PASSOVER
HUNT

by **Tilda Balsley**

Illustrated by **Helen Poole**

KAR-BEN
PUBLISHING

A to Z

An alphabet Passover scene.

Find all the letters in between!

matzah

*Look for the answers to all the puzzles on page 32

Baby Moses

Baby Moses safe afloat.

On the Nile, what was his boat?

Chametz

Not a crumb is left about.

What are the foods that we clean out?

Dayenu

We sing our favorite song.

For which guest did it last too long?

Egypt

Where is Egypt? Do you know?

Passover started there, long ago.

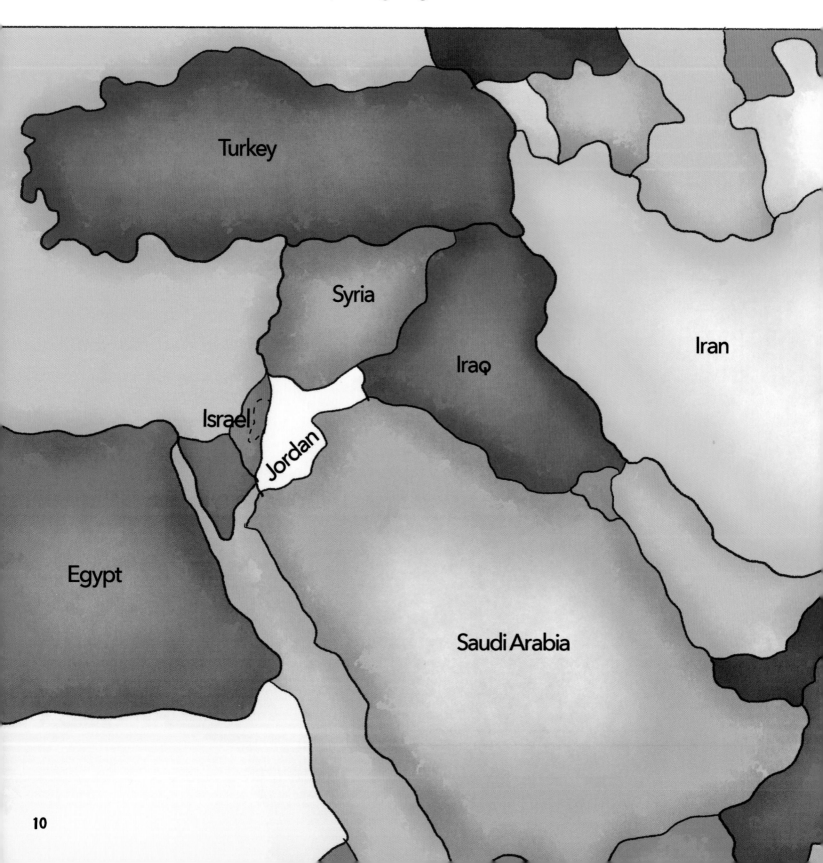

Fiery bush

Flames leap up in Moses' face.

What made this spot a holy place?

God's command

"Go!" said God to Moses. "Go!"

Was Moses' first answer "YES" or "NO"?

SIDDUR

The Story of Queen Esther

In the beginning God created...

The Four Questions

1. ~~~~~~~~~
2. ~~~~~~~~~
3. ~~~~~~~~~
4. ~~~~~~~~~

Haggadah

Which of these tells the Passover tale,

Including the plagues of boils and hail?

Israelites

They were slaves of mean Pharaoh.

What made him say, "Yes, you may GO!"?

Passover

Season of Freedom

Festival of Matzah

Festival of Spring

Festival of Lights

Jewish

The Jewish story of liberation.

What do we **NOT** call this celebration?

kiddush

This comes early in our seder.

Name some things that we'll do later.

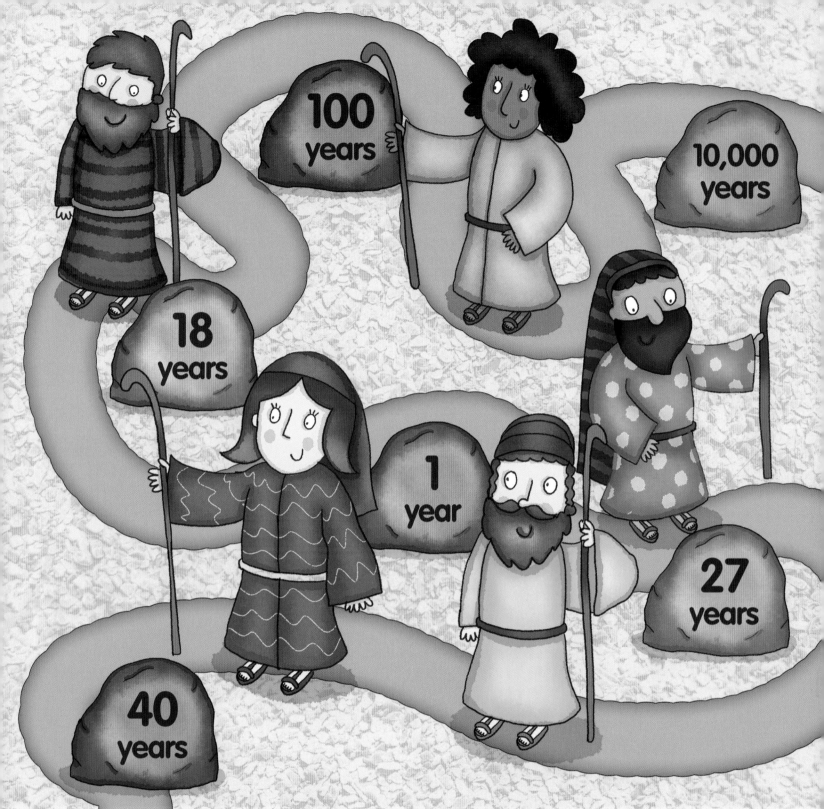

Land of Israel

At last the Jews had found their home,

How many long years did they roam?

Mountain

Moses climbed a mountain high,

Which of these is Mt. Sinai?

Nisan

This is the month that Passover's in.

On which day does it begin?

open door

An open door, an an empty chair.

Who is the guest we welcome there?

Moses

Wandering sheep

Pharaoh

The prophet Elijah

Passover

We celebrate with foods and song.

Point to the things that don't belong.

Questions

Four Questions: Who will ask among us?

In this family, who's the youngest?

Red Sea

As Jews crossed the Red Sea on dry land,

What was Moses holding in his hand?

Slavery

We're slaves no more, and glad, no doubt!

What did the slaves complain about?

Ten Commandments

In the desert God gave us ten rules profound.

On what did Moses write them down?

Unleavened bread

On Passover, matzah is all we eat!

What's your favorite matzah treat?

matzah pizza

matzah with jelly

matzah brei

matzah ball soup

matzah lasagna

matzah toffee

matzah sandwich

vegetables

Bitter herbs and charoset.

On the seder plate what did we forget?

Wine

L'chaim! L'chaim! Our cups we clink.

How many glasses do the grown-ups drink?

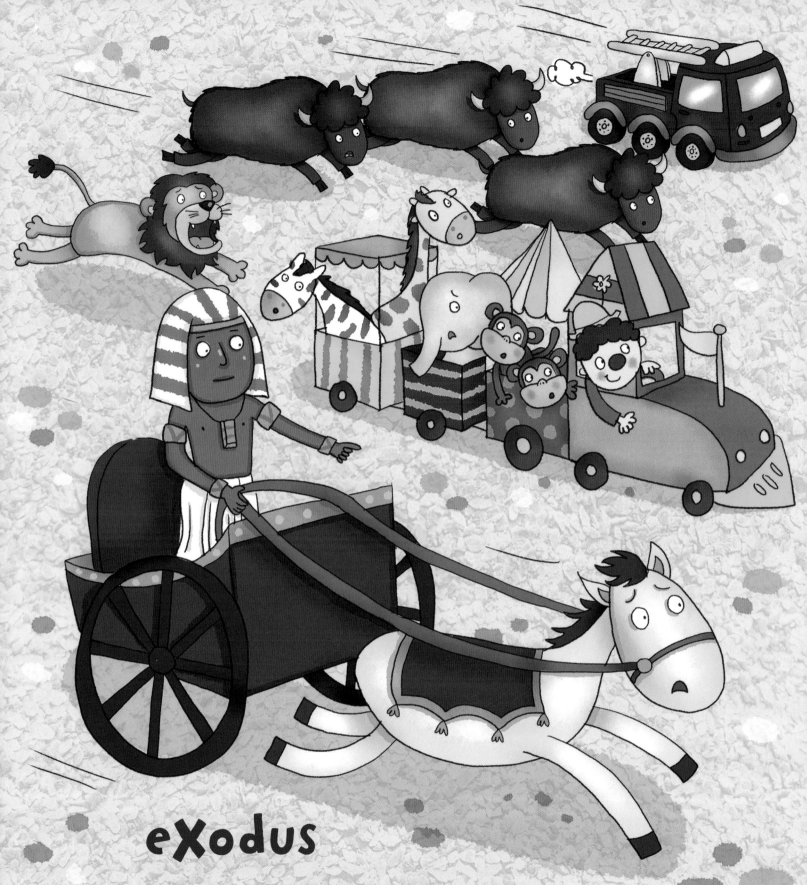

eXoduS

The Jews left Egypt in a flurry,

Who followed close and made them hurry?

YOU

You can help — hunt far and near

To find the afikomen here.

Z'man cheruteinu

We celebrate that we are free!

Happy Passover to every family!

ABOUT PASSOVER

Passover celebrates the exodus of the Israelite slaves from Egypt and the birth of the Jewish people as a nation. The spring holiday begins with a festive meal called a seder. Families gather to read the Haggadah, a book which tells the story of the Jewish people's journey from slavery to freedom. The seder follows a special order. Children ask Four Questions about the rituals, and search for a hidden matzah called the afikomen. Symbolic foods recall the bitterness of slavery, the hurry in which the Jews left Egypt, and the joy of freedom. During the holiday week no leavened food, such as bread is eaten. Matzah takes the place of bread.

ANSWER KEY

6 . . . .

8 . . . .

9 . . . .

10 . . . .

11 . . . .

12 . . . .

13 . . . .

14 . . . .

15 . . . . Festival of Lights

16 . . . . Wash our hands—Bless the matzah—Dip greens in salt water—Read the Passover story—Eat the Passover meal

17 . . . . 40 years

18 . . . .

19 . . . . 15 X

20 . . . .

21 . . . .

22 . . . .

23 . . . .

24 . . . .

25 . . . .

26 . . . . Pick your favorite matzah treat

27 . . . .

28 . . . .

29 . . . .

30 . . . .